To Arnold, Loretha & the Lucky Nine.
—N.J.J.

To my whole family and my students;
past, present, and future. I love you.
—C.M.

Text copyright © 2020 Nancy Johnson James
Illustration copyright © 2020 Constance Moore

Book design by Melissa Nelson Greenberg

Library of Congress Cataloging-in-Publication Data available.
ISBN: 978-1-944903-98-5

Printed in China

10 9 8 7 6 5 4 3 2 1

Cameron Kids is an imprint of Cameron + Company

Cameron + Company
Petaluma, California
www.cameronbooks.com

BR♥WN

by Nancy Johnson James

illustrated by Constance Moore

cameron kids

My mama's brown is chocolate.
It's clear, dark, and sweet.

My daddy's brown is an autumn leaf,
or like a field of wheat.

Brother's brown is cinnamon.
It's spicy and so warm.

Sister's brown like polished pine—
fragrant, tall, and strong.

Auntie's brown is desert sand,
moving with the wind.

Uncle's brown like coffee beans,
a dark and fragrant blend.

My cousins are just babies,
all smiles and curly hair.

Two are like brown sugar . . .

And one, a copper teddy bear.

Granny's brown like honey,

and Papa's caramel.

And my brown is gingerbread.
When we bake I love the smell.

My family has so many browns.
We're different and the same.

I love to paint our
shades of skin,

and give each
one a name.

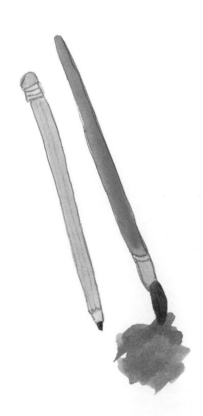

brown

copper

lite
brown

tan

cinamon

dark
brown

tea and
milk

coffee

hot
coco

carmel

choclate

svede

butter
scotch

pine

honey